Sharing Our Truths

Tapwe

Fifth House Publishers
A Fitzhenry & Whiteside Company
195 Allstate Parkway, Markham,
Ontario, L3R 4T8 1-800-387-9776
www.fifthhousepublishers.ca

Published in the United States by
Fifth House Publishers
311 Washington Street
Brighton, Massachusetts 02135

Canada Council for the Arts / Conseil des Arts du Canada

ONTARIO ARTS COUNCIL
CONSEIL DES ARTS DE L'ONTARIO
50 YEARS OF ONTARIO GOVERNMENT SUPPORT OF THE ARTS
50 ANS DE SOUTIEN DU GOUVERNEMENT DE L'ONTARIO AUX ARTS

Cover and interior design by Kerry Designs

Photography by Tessa Macintosh

Additional photographs and illustrations by: page 2, A 50-foot Scow Shooting a Rapid, NWT Archives, C.W. Mathers Fonds, N-1979-058-0019; page 4, *Three Feathers* set, Sarah Pruys, South Slave Divisional Education Council, 2016; page 9, top, satellite image of beaver dam, bottom, beaver, J.D. McDinnon; page 34, Mindy Willett author photo, Christine Scott.

Series editorial by Meaghan Craven

The type in this book is set in 10-on-15-point Trebuchet Regular and 10-on-13-point Tekton Oblique.

Fifth House Ltd. acknowledges with thanks the Canada Council for the Arts and the Ontario Arts Council for their support of our publishing program. We acknowledge the financial support of the Government of Canada through the Canada Book Fund (CBF) for our publishing activities.

The authors would like to thank the Canada Council for the Arts and the South Slave Divisional Education Council for their support.

Printed in China by Sheck Wah Tong Printing

The three strands in a sweetgrass braid represent the Creator, Mother Earth, and all our relations bound together.

Acknowledgments

Henry and Eileen would like to honour their parents Joseph and Charlotte Jerome and Magloire and Agnes Beaver. They would also like to thank their daughter Joline and their grandchildren, Motega, Nevaeh, Naicha, and Niska, who were so patient with all the pictures and getting the book done.

Mindy, Tessa, Henry, and Eileen would all like to say a huge mahsi cho and shout out to Richard Van Camp. Richard gave such enthusiastic support for this book and project. At pertinent times, when Mindy felt she just wasn't living up to what Henry and Eileen deserved, Richard gave her the support and confidence to keep going.

We would like to thank Dot Van Vliet for creating the map. Thank you, Vance Sanderson for the translations from English to Cree throughout the book. We all also want to thank Brent Kaulback and the South Slave Divisional Education Council for their financial and ongoing support. Brent has been an amazing supporter of Indigenous languages for many years. Check out the movie *Three Feathers*, which features Henry and Eileen as actors.

We would like to thank Francois and Leslie Paulette for the incredible opportunity to join in a sweat at their welcoming home in Smith's Landing. Thanks to Pauleen Gordon and Mike Beaver for their hospitality and the opportunity to share in a bison harvest.

We would like to thank Damian and Ingrid Panayi for giving feedback throughout different stages of the writing process. During the drafting phase, Ms. Boggis and her students at Kay Tay Whee School in Dettah, NWT, shared their enthusiasm and ideas. We hope you see your influence in the final version! Mahsi cho to students Trevor Betsina, Tanisha Charlo, Jenna Charlo-Lafferty, Denaze Drygeese-Yelle, Madison Liske, Ryder Manuel, Cameron Martin, Phoenix Miersch, Alphonse Tobie, and Aurthor Tobie-Norn.

Mindy is especially grateful for her supportive husband Damian and their beautiful children, Jack and Rae. Jack and Rae were three and one in 2003 when Mindy and Tessa started *The Land is Our Storybook* series. Our wonderful editor, Meaghan Craven, has been with us for that entire journey. This series would not be the same without her careful and thoughtful suggestions.

Tessa would like to gratefully acknowledge her son Alex for his courageous personal journey in the past few years. She would like to congratulate her daughter Ori and son-in-law Cullen on the birth of their son, Adze. And then there were three!

For our youngest son Jonathan (Jon) who lives in the United States with his wife Megan and their three children Mission, Miyosiw, and Braivry, and also for Jon's oldest son Jaden Saskamoose who lives in Saskatoon with his mother Pamela. For our children Stephan, Henry Jr., and Cynthia who live in Fort Smith, and for our youngest daughter Joline who lives in Edmonton with her husband Cawley and their four children Motega, Nevaeh, Naicha, and Niska.

Sharing Our Truths

Tapwe

by HENRY BEAVER and MINDY WILLETT
with EILEEN BEAVER
photographs by TESSA MACINTOSH

FIFTH HOUSE

Words for Identity

In this book, Henry and Eileen refer to themselves in different ways. Henry identifies as Nehiyaw or Cree. Eileen identifies as Dene Dédlįne. She also sometimes calls herself Dene, or Chipewyan, or Chip. Non-Indigenous people have referred to Indigenous people in Canada as: Aboriginal, Eskimo, First Nations, Indian, Inuit, and Native. For some Indigenous people, these terms are insulting, while others still identify with one or more of them. It's always best to ask someone how they identify themselves.

Tanse,

Henry Beaver *niya. Ni'nehiyawin.* I am Henry Beaver. I am Cree. My parents were Agnes and Magloire Beaver. My wife Eileen is Cree and Chipewyan.

We have three sons and two daughters. When the children were small, we raised them on the land. We don't call the land "the bush"; we call it home. We wanted our children to know their culture and to be proud of who they are.

Canada has not always treated Indigenous people with fairness and respect. Both Eileen and I are survivors of residential schools. But that does not define who we are. We've kept our traditions and our languages, and the government did not get what it wanted—to make us like white Canadians.

The Truth and Reconciliation Commission has challenged Canada to do better so we can recognize and love our differences and learn to live well together.

We can't tell you what to do with the truths we share in this book, but we hope that reading our story will help you get to know us a little better so that together we can make this nation a place we can all be proud of.

Henry Beaver

The background picture is a beaver hide tanned by Eileen Beaver.

Welcome Home

Our youngest daughter Joline lives in Edmonton with her husband Cawley and their four children, Motega, Nevaeh, Naicha, and Niska. In the spring, Joline and the children drove fourteen hours to visit us here in Fort Smith. Eileen and I were excited to spend time with our grandchildren. We wanted to teach them some things about their culture and who they are.

Fort Smith is known as Thebacha, "below the rapids," in Chipewyan. The Slave River flows alongside the community and is home to many pelicans in the summer. The town was built here because the river was a transportation link between southern Canada and the Northwest.

The early fur traders in Fort Smith followed a route that Indigenous people had been using for centuries. Many Cree people from farther south took part in the fur trade and moved north and west with the traders.

Fort Smith is the most southerly community in the NWT. It has about 2,500 residents. Dene, Cree, Inuvialuit, Métis, and non-Indigenous peoples live together here.

Henry is a member of the Salt River First Nation #195. Henry has been the chief three times since 1973. He strongly believes in his treaty rights.

When they arrived, we made a big list of things to do. Motega, the adventurer, wanted to go for a boat ride and trap a beaver. Nevaeh, ever watchful, wanted to learn more about traditional medicines. Quiet Naicha didn't tell us what he wanted to do, and little Niska was a bit squeamish about being out of the city, but both younger boys tried everything. They all wanted to spend time with their cousins and friends.

Motega loves Fort Smith's skateboard park and riding the quad.

To celebrate the solstice, Fort Smith has a handgames tournament. Two teams play, taking turns hiding objects in their hands and guessing which hand the objects are in. During the games, there is loud drumming and singing, and the hiding team uses movements and hand gestures to fool the guessing team.

Eileen and I have spent our lives sharing our cultures with others. We work very hard to ensure our languages are alive. We hope our grandchildren will learn their languages, even though they don't live near us.

Aurora College has a campus in Fort Smith. Henry is often asked to share his knowledge with the college students.

Henry and Eileen acted in Three Feathers*, a movie directed by Carla Ulrich and based on a book by Fort Smith author Richard Van Camp. The actors had to know their lines in Chipewyan, Cree, South Slave, and English!*

Henry and Eileen have helped the South Slave Divisional Education Council publish many books and apps in Cree and Dene Dédlįne (Chipewyan).

Eileen retired in 2016 after twelve years of teaching Indigenous language classes and a cultural program about the amazing stories, rich histories, and rules for living that are important to her people. She also shared the teachings of the medicine wheel.

Maskihkiy Otihtipipayiw (The Medicine Wheel)

The medicine wheel has four parts, each with many teachings. The medicine wheel represents all people. To be a healthy person you must take care of yourself: emotionally, spiritually, physically, and mentally. The medicine wheel also teaches about ideas important to living in this world. Only some of them are included on this wheel.

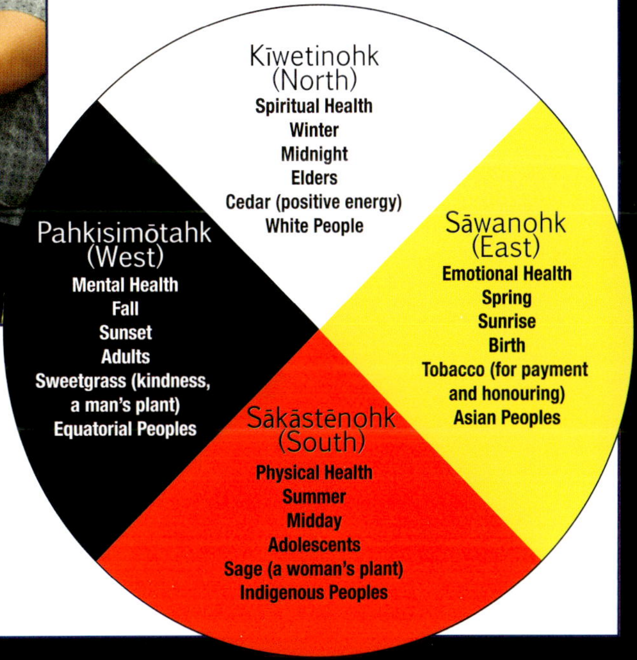

There are apps for each of the territory's nine official Indigenous languages. Eileen's voice is featured on the Chipewyan app. Even when Nevaeh is in Edmonton, she can learn the language from her grandmother.

Tablets and storybooks in the classroom are okay, but the best place to teach our grandchildren is on the land. As many of our Elders say, "Our land is our storybook."

Soon after Joline and the children arrived, my sister asked me to get her some salt. Not salt from the local grocery store but special salt from the land. This would be my chance to show my grandchildren the beautiful Salt Plains and teach them the protocols for harvesting salt.

*Henry and Motega offer tobacco to the land as **reciprocity** for the salt they will harvest.*

Only Indigenous people can legally harvest salt from the plains because the salt is in a national park and is part of traditional lands. Salty water rises to the surface from deep underground, and when the water evaporates, salt crystals remain on the ground.

The plains are home to many unique plants and animals that can live in a salty environment. Bear, bison, lynx, wolf, and the endangered whooping crane lick the salt for its nutrients.

Whose print do you think is beside Naicha's hand? **See page 32 for the answer!**

When you walk across the plains in bare feet, your skin absorbs the nutrients in the salt. Henry's daughter Cynthia has a skin disease called scleroderma. She is strong and uses many medicines from the land to fight her illness. Walking on the Salt Plains is one way she fights her disease.

The salt has always been important to the people of this land. They use it as medicine and to flavour and preserve food. They also traded salt for other necessities offered by other Indigenous people and European traders.

Nevaeh shares the salt harvest with Maggie Sikyea, Henry's sister. She, like many Elders, relieves pain by soaking in a salt bath.

After our trip to the Salt Plains, Motega was eager to take the boat out to trap a beaver. I decided to take all the kids. I wanted to show them how to be respectful while harvesting beaver. The beaver is a very important animal for us. We smoke the meat and we use the fur to keep us warm. My people are great trappers, and long ago we travelled great distances to trap beavers so we could trade their pelts at the forts for things we needed like pots and bullets. One of the reasons my ancestors settled near Fort Smith was to be closer to the trading post here.

Motega drives the boat up the Slave River toward the Salt River to check the beaver trap Henry set the day before.

Henry explains how he set the trap. He uses willow or poplar as bait.

Henry and the children pull the heavy beaver from the water.

The Giant Beaver Dam

Told by Henry Beaver

My dad said that a long time ago, way back in the valley between the Caribou Mountains, the people would cross a beaver dam to go hunting. One time, when they were on the other side of the valley, the dam broke so the people got stuck and couldn't get back. The water was too high. The Elders got together and asked the beavers to build a new bridge so they could get across. They only had to wait three nights because the beavers were such hard workers. Even to this day, when we pass this dam, we make an offering of something important to the beavers. We leave matches or tobacco to show respect and say thanks for helping our ancestors get back to their people. That dam the beavers built is still there. It is the biggest dam in the world at nearly a kilometre long. The dam is so big you can even see it on a satellite photo.

This is an aerial photo of the beaver dam. It is in Wood Buffalo National Park. The leading edge at the top of the photo shows where the dam is now. The beavers only work on part of the dam at any given time. It contains two beaver lodges.

Legend

- Direction of water flow
- Length of the beaver dam
- Beaver lodges

Even though beavers have small hands, they work hard and accomplish much. The smallest of us can finish big tasks if we work hard.

When we brought the beaver home Joline got to work skinning it. I feel good that she can show her children our traditions.

The kids are a bit shy to touch the beaver, at first. Eventually they become more comfortable, especially Motega.

Niska is interested in the beaver tail. He learns how to put it on a stick and roast it over the fire. When the skin is peeled off, the tail is a real treat—even better than the deep-fried dough sprinkled with sugar known as a beaver tail in southern Canada!

Henry inherited his mother's and father's traditional scraping tools. These bone tools have scraped many hides. If they could talk, they would be a Wikipedia of stories and knowledge.

Behind the pictures on this page is a big picture of a moose hide, fur removed. This is the kind of hide used to make moccasins.

Eileen was asked to prepare a few hides for the Three Feathers movie set, so she has a lot of work to do.

Eileen uses beaver fur to make warm mitts and to trim moccasins and parkas that help her and her family stay warm in the cold northern winters.

Eileen is happy to have Joline and Nevaeh around to help. Nevaeh is very keen to learn how to prepare the hide.

Setting Up a Mikiwawhp (Tipi)

Some of my best memories are of lying in the tipi, listening to my family tell stories as I fell asleep. I want my grandchildren to feel what I've felt and to learn the tipi teachings.

1 *Harvest black spruce trees that grow close together as these trees grow straight and are light. Select trees that are taller than your tipi canvas. The longer the trees, the bigger the tipi.*

2 *Cut live trees in the early spring and scrape them when they are still wet. If you cut live trees running with sap, the bark will come off easily. Remove the bark and the limbs and branches or they will tear your canvas. After you've scraped them, let them sit and dry for a few weeks or the sap will weep out and stick to your canvas.*

3 *When the poles are dry, select the ones you want to use. You always need an odd number of poles because odd numbers represent Mother Earth. Each tipi pole has a teaching. For our tipi, we use fifteen poles.*

4 *Make a circle on the ground to help guide you as you place the poles. Then, choose the three strongest poles to form a tripod.*

5 *Lay the three poles beside each other. They should be the same height. Using a rope that's 2–3 metres long, tie the poles together at the top with a clove-hitch knot. Choose a fourth strong pole, and put it aside. This will be your lifting pole.*

6 *The tripod is made of the three strongest poles and reminds us of a family. If the tripod is strong, the family will be strong. Lift the three poles up, with the clove-hitch knot in the air. Place the bottom of each pole, with equal distances between them, on the circle you marked out. The rope that fastens the tripod should hang down toward the centre of the circle.*

How to Tie a Clove-Hitch Knot

The clove-hitch knot attaches a rope to a pole. This knot is strong and won't slip if the pull is straight out from the knot.

1. Make two loops with your rope. They should be the same size. Pass A in front of B.

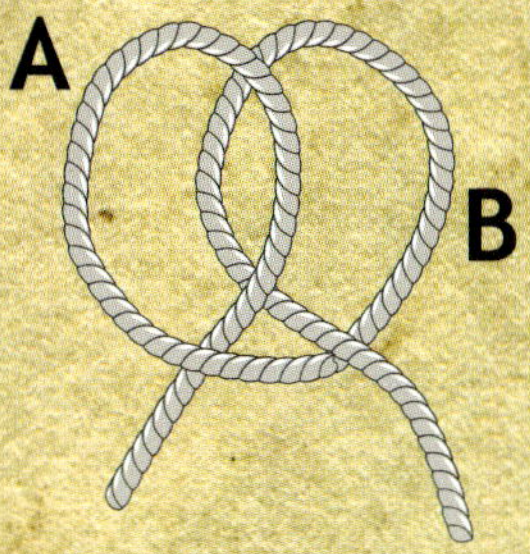

2. Place it over the end of your pole.

3. Pull both ends tight.

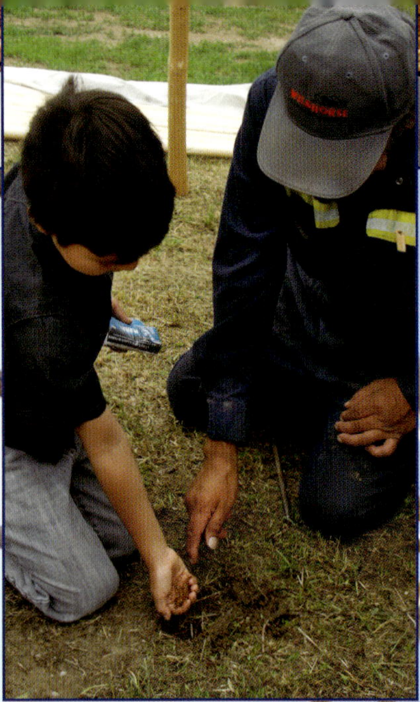

7 *Place tobacco in the centre of the circle where the fire ring will go. Pray as you do this, and think about what you want the tipi to do for you. Henry prays that his grandchildren will each take what they need from the teachings and stories.*

8 *Start to place the remaining poles, leaning them on the tripod poles. They should all rest on the strength of the first three. Remember, the family is the foundation. The other poles represent all our relations. We are all connected by relationships, and we depend on each other.*

9 *Now, take the rope hanging down and walk around the outside of the poles, fastening the poles together. Walk in the direction the sun travels—sun-wise, from east to west. The rope binds the poles and is like our sacred bonds to each other.*

10 *Take your lifting pole and bind the canvas to it very tightly so it doesn't slip.*

11 *Lift the pole and walk the canvas around the poles to spread the canvas and form the tipi.*

12 *When the canvas is in place, use pegs to nail it into the ground.*

I'm glad when my family helps me make a tipi as it can be tough work, especially when the wind is strong. We are like the poles because we need each other for support.

When the tipi was ready, we laid down spruce boughs inside it. The smell was so wonderful that as soon as we entered the tipi, we felt good.

After an offering of tobacco, the family harvests many boughs.

The tipi door should face east, toward the rising sun, the beginning of the day. East also reminds us of the beginning of creation.

When the boughs were down, it was time to make the sacred fire circle. As I brought them into the tipi, I thanked each of the grandfather rocks my family has used and reused. These rocks are the library of life as they listen to and keep all our stories. We think of rocks as having living spirits.

Our Words

amisk	beaver
askiy kiteyemiht	honouring the land, "paying the land"
kayās asiniy	grandfather rocks
kihci iskotew	sacred fire
maskihkiy otihtipipayiw	medicine wheel
mikiwahp	tipi
mostosowēhkask	sage
nimosom	grandfather
nosisimak	grandchildren
ohkoma (kokom)	grandmother
oskwatim	beaver dam
sîwîhtâkân	salt from the land
wēhkaskwa	sweetgrass

Henry teaches Motega about the grandfather rocks as he places them in each of the four directions.

When everyone in the family participates, they can laugh and share stories together.

It took us a few days to prepare the tipi, and then the kids were excited to get inside and roast some marshmallows over the fire. Now that the tipi was ready, we could smudge and share some stories.

Smudging

As Told by Eileen Beaver

I was born and raised a Roman Catholic. My grandfather taught me that I need to learn to walk in two cultures. "You are both," he said. "You have the choice to be the best of each of you." I used to get so mad at white people for what happened to our people—for taking generations of children away to residential schools and for taking all the best parts of our land. But my grandfather used to say, "You have to stop that because then you're angry at yourself too." He reminded me that I'm Chip from him but I also have Cree, French, Métis, and Irish within me, so I shouldn't call myself down. Smudging each day helps me to walk a good path.

Smudging is one way to cleanse our spirits. To clean our physical bodies, we take a bath. To clean our spirits, we smudge by burning sacred plants in our homes and near our bodies. Our spirits are bigger than our bodies. When we are around others, we can pick up their negative thoughts and emotions. Smudging can help us get rid of negative things and remind us to have good, positive thoughts. There are many sacred plants used in smudging, but the four main ones are: cedar, sage, sweetgrass, and tobacco. I usually burn sage when I smudge.

Eileen takes her hair out of her braid to smudge.

Sacred Plants

Sage is a woman's plant. Even if a woman is in her moontime she can smudge using sage. It's often used in public ceremonies so everyone can take part.

Tobacco is used to pay the earth. When we take something from the land, we offer tobacco in exchange. It helps us to pause and be grateful.

Cedar blesses. When I go on a fast, I place bundles of cedar nearby to help clear my mind.

Sweetgrass is a man's plant. There are seven blades of grass in each of the three strands of a sweetgrass braid. They bring together the father, the mother, and all our relations. When I want to give sweetgrass to someone, I put my prayers for that person into the sweetgrass while I am making the braid. When they burn the braid, my prayers are released.

I use an **abalone shell** as a container for the plants when I smudge. It doesn't come from our land, but our people have always traded with other Indigenous peoples.

The Creator's favourite bird is the eagle. As Henry smudges, Eileen holds an eagle feather to help his prayers reach the Creator.

I've been an Elder in training for twenty years. I am always learning, but I also try to teach what I have learned. There is no wrong way to smudge. We never say, "This is the only way." We don't have a lot of rules. But we do want to be sincere about what we are doing. Smudging is for all people, every colour and every culture. It reminds us to be humble and think of others.

Henry tells his grandchildren that their thoughts are between them, the Creator, and Mother Earth.

When Eileen teaches her grandchildren, she shares only what each of them is ready to hear, as they are all at different stages. She lets them experience their new knowledge, and tells a little bit more each time she sees them. Here she is teaching Niska to start smudging at his crown.

How to Smudge

If you want to try smudging, put sage in a container like a shell. Light the sage. When the smoke rises, use your hands to help it flow over your body. As you do this, pray with intent. Begin by cleansing your head, also called your crown. This is your connection to the Creator. Thank the Creator for your blessings. Smudging is powerful, so be specific about what you're thankful for.

Joline helps Nevaeh by smudging her back.

When you cleanse your eyes, think about how you'll see clearly throughout the day, looking for beauty in each person you interact with. Cleanse your mouth so you speak truthfully and with kind words that will not hurt others. Cleanse your throat so you can sing, your stomach so your inner powers are strong. Thank your knees for carrying you through each day, and then move along, all the way down to your feet.

Nevaeh shares that when she smudges, it smells good and makes her feel safe.

Nevaeh finishes by bringing her hands to her heart. She cleanses her heart and gives prayers of thanks and a request to have good thoughts throughout the day.

The four sacred plants are not the only important ones. I want my grandchildren to know that the land offers many plant medicines. We use all sorts of plants for many different reasons. Who knows? Maybe someday we won't have a pharmacy nearby. It's important to know about the medicines from the land. Only trained people should use plant medicines. You have to know what you're doing because plants can be very powerful and may harm you if you use them incorrectly.

Wild Roses are beautiful. The rose bush stems were traditionally used to make straight, light arrows. The petals and rosehips are high in vitamin C. We collect the petals and put them in a glass jug of water. The nutrients in the petals seep out into the water. Put this rose-petal water on your skin to make it soft.

Dandelion ***roots*** *and leaves are good for you. Harvest pesticide-free dandelions. The greens can go in salads. You can eat the roots as you would a potato, or you can dry them. Some people drink dandelion-root tea instead of coffee. The roots are good for your pancreas, liver, and gall bladder.*

White poplar is a natural bug repellant. When the mosquitoes are bad, rub the poplar tree bark powder on your face. This powder is also a mild sunscreen.

The spruce tree has given our people many things. Spruce gum is high in vitamin C. It is also a medicine for some types of cancer. The gum is an antibiotic and can be a salve to put on skin infections. Springtime spruce tips taste lemony and can be made into a tea that helps with colds and flu.

Chaga is a wild fungus found on living birch trees. Some people call it the king of medicinal mushrooms. Henry shares with Naicha how to harvest chaga. When made into a tea, it can bring down swelling. It brings balance to where you need it and is known to be good for cancers. In Cree, chaga is called pōhskan.

Just being out on the land together is good medicine.

When I was young, the solstice was important to our family. We would stay up all night sharing stories. Since our grandchildren were with us, we decided to spend the night in our new tipi doing the same.

Eileen shares the moose antlers story with the family.

The sucker fish's jaw bone. What does it look like to you?

This photo was taken on June 21 at around 10:30 p.m. at the Slave River rapids. Fort Smith is below the Arctic Circle, so it is not quite far enough north to experience the midnight sun on solstice.

Our Stories: How The Female Moose Lost Her Beautiful Antlers

As Told by Eileen Beaver

A long time ago, animals had the power to do anything they wanted. Animals could talk, trees could talk, even the grass and rocks could talk—they still do, but most of us don't know how to listen. Back then, both male and female moose had antlers. They loved their antlers. They were proud of their antlers. At that time, they were allowed to take them off, but only if they watched over them. One spring, a male and female moose came down by the river to eat, just as the sun was coming up. They were wading in the water because they loved the water plants—the fresh, juicy, and crunchy underwater plants. But, this one morning, the female moose was getting impatient when the plants got caught on her antlers. She said, "I'm just going to rest my antlers on the rocks over there while I eat."

The male moose said, "No. Creator says we're not allowed to. We're supposed to take care of our things and care for our bodies." "It will be okay," she replied. "If anything happens, it will be your fault," he warned.

She took off her beautiful but heavy antlers and laid them on a rock, thinking, "It'll be all right. It's just while I enjoy my breakfast."

Meanwhile, a sucker fish was running up the river. Sucker saw the beautiful antlers on the rock and thought, "I'm going to play a trick on her." Sucker fish twirled and jumped up and got a wee bit bigger. He twirled and jumped up again, and again got a wee bit bigger. He twirled and jumped up again, and again got a wee bit bigger. Each twirl and jump got him just a bit bigger until he was big enough to grab the antlers with his mouth and jump back into the water. They were so big that they hurt his mouth so he quickly tried to reverse his twirling to regain his small size. As he shrunk, the antlers shrunk too, and they were stuck inside his mouth.

To this day the animals must pay for their ways. Sucker paid for his mischievousness. The Creator made him keep the heavy antlers in his mouth. So, sucker fish can't chew; they can only suck. This reminds them (and us) not to steal from others. The male moose must lose his antlers every year and grow them back. This is a reminder to help your friends when they are making bad choices. When the female moose calls she sounds like she's crying because she is brokenhearted and wants her beautiful antlers back. From the day that moose left her antlers on the rock, female moose have not had antlers. This reminds us to look after the gifts the Creator has given us.

Just as the female moose should have taken care of her antlers, we are taught to take care of ourselves. Many of our people have long hair, including men and boys. Our hair represents our strength, the strength of our family, and our relationship with the earth. Our Elders tell us that we must respect everything in our lives: the animals, our friends and family, ourselves, and our hair.

The children are curious about the teachings, so Henry shares a story too.

Our Stories: The Twins

As Told by Henry Beaver

A long time ago, there lived twin brothers. They were very close. They played together, and though they sometimes fought, they were best friends. They were inseparable. They used to go down to the river to bathe every morning.

That's where they braided their hair, smudged, and said their morning prayers. They knew the teachings about respecting their hair, but they didn't always listen.

The twins were warriors too. When they became adults, they went to fight another tribe that had attacked theirs. One of the brothers died in the battle.

The other brother went back home and each morning would go to the river, but now in sadness. Even four years later, he was still grieving for his brother. He was also angry. One morning when he was combing his hair by the river he could see a spirit walking toward him, bent over. He was tattered and dirty. He was walking closer and closer through the water. As he got closer, the pitiful spirit said, "Brother, is that you?" "Yes, my brother, it is me, but what has happened to you? Why are you so dirty? Is it so bad in the spirit world?"

"Remember when we didn't listen to the Elders? Knowing what we were supposed to do and yet choosing not to listen? I now must walk this world until I have collected every hair that I didn't respect.

Henry keeps each hair he loses in a bundle. Even when he gets a haircut, he puts down a towel to collect each hair. He burns the collected strands to save himself from walking all over Earth for years after dying.

Also, the longer you keep holding on to me with your pain the longer I have to wander in-between worlds. You're crying for me and not living the life you're supposed to. If you love me, you have to let me go."

The brother told all the people back at camp about seeing the spirit of his twin. He now knew why we Cree always tell our children to take care of their hair, to burn loose strands in the fire as they say prayers. We also try not to let our loved ones be lost in between two worlds, and we let them go.

This story of the brothers reminds us to live a good and respectful life. Just like the sweetgrass braid, when your hair is braided, your mind, your body, and your spirit are brought together as one. To be a whole person, you must take care of all your parts.

The morning after our night in the tipi, we talked about the teachings we had given during the visit. What lessons do you think my grandchildren learned from their experiences with us?

Each morning Henry braids Eileen's hair. He puts prayers in the braid. The braid then holds good thoughts for her all day. What else did the children learn about the sweetgrass braid and braid of hair?

What did Motega learn from the grandfather rocks and the placement of the tipi door?

What did Nevaeh learn about plants, medicines, and the protocols around harvesting?

What did Niska learn about beavers?

What does Naicha think about being on the land?

What did Joline learn about working hard together?

When it's time for them to leave, we give each of our beautiful grandchildren a big hug.

Tapwe means “it is so” or “the truth.” We have shared some of our truths with you. We don’t have a word for goodbye in our languages. Instead we say wapuntun asumina. We’ll see you again.

Wapuntun asumina.

All the Details

Salt Plains and Wood Buffalo National Park

The Salt Plains are part of Wood Buffalo National Park which was created in 1922 to protect the last herds of wood bison in northern Canada. It is a UNESCO World Heritage Site and one of Canada's largest national parks. The plains are home to many animals including bear, bison, lynx, wolf, and whooping crane.

Who Are the Nēhiyaw or Cree?

The Cree form one of the largest groups of Indigenous people in North America with over 200,000 people. In Canada, most Cree live west of Lake Superior in Ontario, Manitoba, Saskatchewan, and Alberta, but also in the southern part of the Northwest Territories. The Cree language has many speakers and many variations including Henry's dialect, Bush Cree.

The Salt River First Nation (SRFN)

Henry is a member and former chief of the Salt River First Nation. The Salt River First Nation is made up of Cree and Chipewyan who descended from Indigenous people who traditionally used and lived on land in the Slave River area.

The Salt River First Nation (SRFN) Treaty Settlement Agreement (TSA) was signed in 2002. The agreement is between the SRFN and Canada. It lays out the responsibilities the government has to the SRFN and its traditional lands, which were first described when Treaty 8 was signed in 1899. This agreement relates to the land in and around Fort Smith, as well as land within Wood Buffalo National Park.

Animals of the Salt Plains and Their Tracks

Bear – muskwa (This is the print you can see in the picture on page 6!)

Beaver – amisk

Lynx – pisiw

Wolf – mahihkan

Whooping crane – ota cháhk

1899 2001 SALT RIVER FIRST NATION

Glossary

Fast — to stop eating or drinking for a period of time.

Land of the Midnight Sun — the place where the sun does not set in the summer time (above the Arctic Circle [66 0 33']). While Fort Smith is below the Arctic Circle the sun is up for almost 19 hours on June 21. How long is it up where you live?

Moontime — the period of menstruation. It is called this because, like the full moon, it generally occurs once a month.

Protocol — the traditions or customs of a community or people. Each Indigenous community has its own protocols. It is important to ask what the protocols are to show respect.

Reciprocity — in exchange for. For example, the land gives life, so in reciprocity, Henry gives tobacco to the land. Henry shares stories, so in exchange, his grandchildren give him thanks and love, and sometimes cookies.

Salve — an ointment or cream that promotes healing.

Summer Solstice — the day of the year with the most sunlight. In Canada, the solstice or, June 21, was declared National Indigenous Peoples Day.

Treaty — a promise or an agreement between two parties or two nations. All Canadians are "treaty people" as it takes all of us to fulfill the treaty promise.

Truth and Reconciliation Commission (TRC) — started in 2008 to document the history and impacts of residential schools. It provided people who attended residential school an opportunity to share their experiences. In 2015 the TRC published 94 "calls to action" about reconciliation (restoring friendly relations) between non-Indigenous Canadians and Indigenous peoples. Find out what you can do. It will take all of us to do what Henry said, "make this country a place we are all proud to call our home."

UNESCO — the United Nations Educational, Scientific and Cultural Organization. The organization promotes peace and security through nations working together. If a place is listed as a UNESCO site, it has special significance for everyone on Earth.

About the Authors and Photographer

Henry and Eileen Beaver are respected Elders who live in Fort Smith, NWT. They have written many books with the South Slave Divisional Education Council, starred in a film called *Three Feathers*, and generously share their knowledge of language, culture, and spiritual practices.

Mindy Willett is a passionate advocate for all things northern. *Sharing Our Truths* is the ninth book she has co-authored with storytellers from across the NWT. Mindy enjoys all the seasons and is most happy when canoeing, cranberry picking, or skiing with her family. She is honoured to have had the chance to learn from Henry and Eileen.

Tessa Macintosh celebrated forty years of living in the North in 2017. She is an award-winning photographer who has worked for *The Native Press* newspaper and the NWT government. She also operates a busy guest house in Yellowknife's Old Town. Tessa is grateful for the amazing families she's met during the past decade working on *The Land Is Our Storybook*. As Mindy says, "Can you believe we're so blessed? Pinch me!"

The Land is Our Storybook

Titles in the series, all co-written by Mindy Willett and illustrated by Tessa Macintosh:

We Feel Good Out Here Julie-Ann Andre
Delta is My Home Tom McLeod
Living Stories Therese Zoe and Philip Zoe
Come and Learn with Me Sheyenne Jumbo
Proud to be Inuvialuit James Pokiak
The Caribou Feed Our Soul Pete Enzoe
At the Heart of It Raymond Taniton
No Borders Darla Evyagotailak
Sharing Our Truths Henry Beaver with Eileen Beaver

The first six titles are also available in French!